I wish I could... ROAR!

A story about self-confidence

Tiziana Bendall-Brunello

Illustrated by John Bendall-Brunello

QED

QED Publishing

"ROAR!" said Daddy Lion.
And all the little animals ran off in fright.

"Squeak!" said Little Lion.

"Not squeak!" said Dad. "We lions ROAR!
Now off you go and practise roaring.
Keep practising... ROAR... ROAR... ROAR!
I know you can do it."

Little Lion decided to practise on his mum.

"Squeak!" he called, pouncing on her.

Squeak!

"It's not squeak!" said Mummy Lion. "It's ROAR!"

"Why don't you ask your brothers and sisters to show you how?"

"ROAR! ROAR! ROAR!
Roar! Roar! Roar!"
All Little Lion's brothers
and sisters were waking up
and roaring loudly.

ROAR!

"Squeak!" tried Little Lion
again. "Squeak, squeak!"

Squeak!

ROAR!

Roar!

Roar!

But the others just laughed at him.
"Not squeak!" they said. "ROAR!"

Little Lion ran away into the long grass.

"I wish I could roar," snuffled Little Lion. "But all I can do is..."

Squeak!

"Squeak!" said Mouse.

"Squeak!" said Little
Lion back to Mouse.

"Why are you squeaking?" asked Mouse.
"You lions roar – you don't squeak!
It's we mice that go squeak!" she said.

"Let me see if I can help you," said Mouse.

Squeak!

"It's no good," sniffled Little Lion. "I can't roar."

"Well, let's see if this helps," said Mouse.
And she whispered softly into his ear,
"ROAR! You can do it! ROAR!"

"Roar!" said Little Lion proudly.

"Hey!" Little Lion's brothers and sisters shouted proudly. "You've learned to roar! Hurrah! Hurrah!"

ROAR!

"We knew you could ROAR!" Daddy and Mummy
Lion said. "You just didn't know that yourself."

"Yes, I can!" said Little Lion triumphantly. "ROAR! ROAR! ROAR!"

Notes for parents and teachers

- Look at the front cover of the book together. Ask the children to name the animal. Can the children guess how the animal feels?

- Can the children understand the meaning of "ROAR" and "SQUEAK"? Show them the differences between a roar and a squeak. For this exercise, focus on your posture and facial expression. Discuss how you feel when you roar and squeak, and how other people may react to these two behaviours.

- Ask the children why Little Lion cries. Discuss reasons for crying and feelings associated with crying. Do the children know the opposite of crying? At this point, it is good to discuss with the children the different types of feelings (e.g. happy, sad) and associated behaviours and facial expressions.

- Ask the children why the other lions laugh at Little Lion. Is it a good thing to laugh when a friend is crying? Discuss ways in which children could help their friends when they cry.

- Can the children name all the animals in the book? Ask them which animal they like the most and why.

- Ask the children to describe what happens to the other animals when Little Lion says "ROAR". How does Little Lion look when he says "ROAR"?

- Ask the children to draw a picture of themselves saying "SQUEAK" and then saying "ROAR".

Consultant: Cecilia A. Essau
Professor of Developmental Psychopathology
Director of the Centre for Applied Research and
Assessment in Child and Adolescent Wellbeing,
Roehampton University, London

Editor: Jane Walker
Designer: Fiona Hajée

Copyright © QED Publishing 2011

First published in the UK in 2011 by
QED Publishing
A Quarto Group Company
226 City Road
London ECIV 2TT

www.qed-publishing.co.uk

A catalogue record for this book is available from the British Library.

ISBN 978 1 84835 674 0

Printed in China